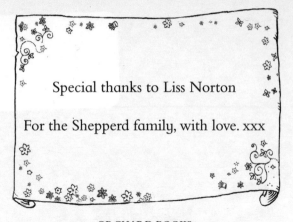

Special thanks to Liss Norton

For the Shepperd family, with love. xxx

ORCHARD BOOKS
Carmelite House
50 Victoria Embankment
London EC4Y 0DZ
Orchard Books Australia
Level 17/207 Kent Street, Sydney, NSW 2000
A Paperback Original

First published in 2015 by Orchard Books

Text © Hothouse Fiction Limited 2015

Illustrations © Orchard Books 2015

A CIP catalogue record for this book is available
from the British Library.

ISBN 978 1 40834 012 7

1 3 5 7 9 10 8 6 4 2

Printed in Great Britain

Orchard Books is a division of Hachette Children's Books,
an Hachette UK company

www.hachette.co.uk

Series created by Hothouse Fiction
www.hothousefiction.com

Mermaid Magic

ROSIE BANKS

ORCHARD

This is the Secret Kingdom

Pearl Shoals School

Contents

A Message from Trixi

"Can I have the butterfly cutter first, please?" asked Summer Hammond.

She was in her kitchen with her best friends, Jasmine Smith and Ellie Macdonald. They were all wearing aprons over their pretty summer dresses, because they were making biscuits for their school bake sale to raise money for new library books.

Jasmine handed it to her. "I'm making star biscuits," she said. "I'm going to sprinkle them with edible glitter when they're cooked so they twinkle like real stars."

Ellie grinned. "That's a great idea! I'm going to use the mermaid cutter and decorate the tails with chocolate buttons."

Summer's two little brothers, Finn and Connor, dashed into the kitchen. "Aren't your biscuits ready yet?" Connor asked, disappointed. "We want to try them."

"You can have a couple of chocolate buttons," Summer said, handing her brothers a few.

"Thanks!" the boys exclaimed. They ran out again, munching happily.

Summer rolled her dough and began cutting out butterfly shapes. She pushed

the kitchen door shut, then said in a low voice, "It's too bad my butterfly biscuits can't fly, like the Catch-Me Cookies we ate in Candy Cove. They'd be the hit of the bake sale!"

The girls exchanged excited looks. Candy Cove was in the Secret Kingdom, a magical land ruled by jolly King Merry. It was full of elves, giants, pixies and other amazing creatures – and the girls loved to visit.

"I wonder when Trixi will come for us," Jasmine said. When they were needed in the Secret Kingdom, their pixie friend, Trixi, always sent them a message through a magic box that they shared.

"Soon, I hope," said Ellie. "I can't wait to see her and King Merry again."

The girls finished cutting out their

biscuits and arranged them on baking
sheets. Ellie popped them in the oven and
Jasmine set the timer. As it began to tick,
she sighed loudly.

"What's wrong?" asked Summer.

"The timer has just reminded me about
Queen Malice's hourglass," Jasmine
replied.

King Merry's mean sister, Queen

Malice, had put a curse on the Secret
Kingdom and as black sand trickled
through her magical hourglass it was
gradually destroying all the good magic
there. It was causing problems across
the land, and once all the sand had run
through there'd be no good magic left in
the kingdom at all.

Ellie shivered. "Remember how horrible
it was in the Secret Kingdom when
Queen Malice took over before?"

"We stopped her then, and we'll stop
her again," said Jasmine determinedly.
"We've already found the Charmed
Heart. Once we find the other three
Enchanted Objects, her curse will be
lifted."

King Merry's ancestors had carefully
hidden four Enchanted Objects in distant

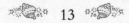

corners of the Secret Kingdom. The girls
were trying to find them all because their
powerful magic would destroy Queen
Malice's curse, but they'd been so well
hidden, so long ago, that even King
Merry didn't know where they were. To
make things worse, Queen Malice was
searching for the objects, too!

"Let's check the Magic Box," suggested
Summer. "Maybe Trixi's sent us a
message."

"Good idea!" agreed Ellie and Jasmine.

The girls raced upstairs to Summer's
bedroom. It was a cosy room with
walls decorated with animal posters
and shelves crammed with books. Ellie
closed the door so Summer's brothers
wouldn't see what they were doing, while
Summer pulled the Magic Box out from

underneath her bed. It was a beautiful
box, carved with mermaids, unicorns
and other magical creatures. A mirror,
surrounded by six glittering gems, was set
into the top.

"The mirror's glowing!" Summer cried
eagerly. She hurriedly set the box on the
bed and they all crowded round.

"Here comes Trixi's riddle," said Jasmine

as words began to appear in the mirror.
She read it out:

"This place of learning lies beneath
The shimmering turquoise sea.
Here long-haired swimmers
Study hard to learn their A B C."

The box opened and a magical map
of the Secret Kingdom floated out. Ellie
caught it and spread it out on Summer's
desk. It was a very special map and
looking at it was almost like peering
through a window into the Secret
Kingdom. The girls could see figures
moving on it – galloping unicorns,
flying dream dragons and skiing Snow
Brownies.

"It's somewhere under the sea," Jasmine

said, "so we need to look around the coast."

Aquamarine waves lapped along the shores of the crescent-shaped kingdom. Some young elves were paddling on a sandy beach near the bottom of the map and colourful boats bobbed on the gentle waves.

"A place of learning must mean a school," said Ellie. "So we're looking for a school under the sea."

"What about the long-haired swimmers?" Summer said thoughtfully. "Fish don't have hair..."

"But mermaids do," Ellie reminded her.

"Of course!" Summer cried.

They all bent low over the map, trying to read the tiny writing.

"Here!" Jasmine exclaimed suddenly.

"Pearl Shoals School." She pointed to a shimmering building under the sea. "That must be the place."

Excitedly the girls placed their hands on the Magic Box. "The answer is Pearl Shoals School," they cried together. They waited expectantly for Trixi to come zooming out of the box on her flying leaf, but there was no sign of her.

"That's weird," said Jasmine. "Trixi always comes when we solve the riddle. Do you think we've got the answer wrong?"

Before Ellie or Summer could reply, they heard a faint knocking. "What's that?" asked Ellie. She glanced round the room, trying to work out what was making the sound.

"It's coming from inside the Magic

Box," Summer said, puzzled. She lifted the lid and Trixi flew out, giggling.

"Here I am!" she cried. "Thanks for letting me out!"

Pearl Shoals School

Trixi twirled around Summer's bedroom on her leaf, leaving a trail of golden sparkles behind her. She wore a cute dress with a pink skirt that was made of flower petals, and a few locks of her blonde hair peeked out from under a matching pink-and-yellow hat. She flew to each of the girls in turn and kissed them on the tips of their noses. "It's lovely to see you all again," she said.

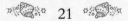

"It's good to see you, too, Trixi," said
Ellie.

"Why couldn't you get out of the box?"
Summer asked.

Trixi's bright smile faded. "My pixie
ring's magic still isn't working very well
because of Queen Malice and her nasty
curse."

"Has King Merry had any ideas about
where the next Enchanted Object might
be?" asked Jasmine eagerly. "Is that why
you've come?"

Trixi smiled again. "Yes. He thinks it's
hidden under the sea."

"Brilliant!" the girls exclaimed together.
They quickly held hands as Trixi tapped
her pixie ring and chanted:

"Mean Queen Malice is causing worry,

So off to Pearl Shoals School, let's hurry!"

A fountain of multi-coloured sparkles
came whooshing out of her ring. They
swirled around the girls like a glittering
whirlpool.

Suddenly Trixi said, "One, two, three…
Jump!"

The girls leapt into the air and landed
with a splash in warm water that reached
up to their ankles.

As the sparkles faded, they saw that
they were on a wide beach with pink
sand. Palm trees were dotted here and
there and bright blue water lapped
about their feet. Tiny glittering fish swam
around them, their scales flashing in the
golden sunshine.

Looking down, Jasmine noticed that

her purple sundress had been transformed into a hot-pink wetsuit dotted with twinkly silver hearts. Her friends' dresses had also been changed into pretty wetsuits. Summer's was yellow with a glittery goldfish on the front, and Ellie's was purple with green stripes like shimmering strands of seaweed. They had matching flippers on their feet, and they were all wearing the beautiful jewelled tiaras that always appeared when they arrived in the Secret Kingdom. These showed that the girls were Very Important Friends of King Merry.

"Nearly ready," Trixi said. "We just need one more thing." She tapped her ring again and chanted:

"We've come to stop the mean

queen's trouble
So give us all a breathing bubble!"

There was a brilliant blue flash and
suddenly a shining bubble surrounded
each of the girls' heads. Trixi was wearing
one, too.

"Perfect," she said. "We'll be able
to breathe and speak to each other

underwater now."

"When we visited Mermaid Reef you did a special spell so we could breathe underwater naturally," Ellie said, puzzled.

"My magic was stronger then," Trixi explained. "But Queen Malice's curse has made it weaker and I don't want to take any chances. These bubbles will keep us extra-safe."

Summer looked round at the sparkling sea, the long stretch of glittering sand and the palm trees with their emerald green leaves. She hated the thought that Queen Malice's nasty curse could spoil all the good magic flowing through this beautiful beach and every other wonderful part of the Secret Kingdom. "Let's start looking for the second Enchanted Object right now," she said.

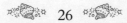

"I know someone who might be able to help us find it," said Trixi.

They waded further out, then dived into the warm, clear water. As they swam down to the sandy seabed, bright fish darted all around them, their scales shimmering.

The girls' flippers made it easy to swim. A very slight kick of their feet sent them

skimming through the water. "This is brilliant!" exclaimed Ellie, performing a perfect back flip. Summer and Jasmine joined in, then they all stopped and stared as a magnificent building came into view. It was built of glistening pearls with tall turrets rising from its four corners. An arched doorway stood at the top of a flight of wide steps.

"Welcome to Pearl Shoals School," said Trixi. "This is where merchildren learn how to do mermaid magic."

"It reminds me of one of those ruined castles you sometimes see in aquariums," said Summer. "But the pearls make it much, much prettier."

"Hello, there," called a tinkling voice. Turning, the girls saw a mermaid swimming towards them. She had long

blonde hair that floated around her in
glistening tresses, a silver tiara and a
sparkling silver tail.

"Lady Merlana!" Jasmine exclaimed
delightedly. They'd met the beautiful
mermaid before when they'd saved the
wishing pearl at Mermaid Reef.

"Hello, girls," Lady Merlana said,

smiling. "And Trixi, too. What a lovely surprise!"

"Are you visiting Pearl Shoals School?" asked Ellie.

"Yes," replied the mermaid. "Some of the pupils are putting on a display of magic in my honour. Why don't you come and watch?"

"We'd love to!" the girls chimed together.

They followed Lady Merlana through the arched doorway and found themselves in a wide hall with a floor of twinkling golden sand and walls of shimmering pearl. Silver light streamed through the high windows, making the whole room shine as though it had been dusted with glitter.

Now a line of little merchildren came

swimming into the room behind a
grown-up mermaid with a beautiful
purple tail. "Sit down, everyone," she said
firmly.

The little mermaids and merboys sat on
a line of sparkling rocks and chattered in
low voices. They looked shyly at the girls
and one of them whispered loudly, "They

have *legs* instead of tails!"

The purple-tailed mermaid swam over eagerly. "Lady Merlana, thank you for coming. The children are very excited about their magic show and have worked hard to perfect it. I see you've brought some friends." Smiling brightly, she turned to the girls, setting her long lilac hair swirling. "I'm Miss Sandy, the teacher here."

"This is Summer, Ellie and Jasmine," said Lady Merlana. "They're friends from the Other Realm. And Trixi is King Merry's royal pixie."

"We're honoured to welcome such important friends," Miss Sandy said, looking at the girls' tiaras. She showed them to a stone bench covered in cushions made from soft, mossy seaweed, then called three of her pupils over.

One of the mermaids had long black hair and a bright pink tail, the second had curly orange hair and a green tail, and the third had blonde hair and a yellow tail. "They look a bit like us," whispered Jasmine with a grin. "Only with tails instead of legs, of course!"

The three little mermaids bowed to Lady Merlana, then they sang a spell in sweet voices:

"A flick of tails, a swirl of hair
And suddenly a bouquet's there!"

They flicked their shimmering tails and a ball of silver light rose up from the seabed. The light turned into a mass of slimy brown seaweed the moment the

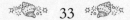

mermaids caught it. "Oh no!" they gasped, throwing it down. "What's happened? We wanted to make flowers for you, Lady Merlana."

Miss Sandy looked shocked. "I'm so sorry, Lady Merlana. Something's gone wrong." She quickly called to two merboys with sparkling blue tails and purple hair, "The rainbow fish spell, now, my dears."

They floated up from their rocks as a shoal of silver fish swam in through one of the open windows. They sang a spell:

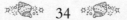

*"Mermaid magic, hear our wish
And change the colour of these fish.
Give them stripes of red, green, blue,
Purple, orange, yellow, too."*

Suddenly the fish were bathed in golden light, but when it vanished they'd changed into ugly, brown pufferfish with bulging cheeks and spiny heads!

The merboys stared in horror and one of them burst into tears.

"I really can't understand it," Miss Sandy said anxiously. "The children have never had trouble with these spells before." She swam over to comfort the two merboys, making the pufferfish dart away.

"Please don't worry," called Summer. "Queen Malice's curse is causing

problems and we've come to Pearl Shoals to help put things right."

"We need to find the next Enchanted Object," said Jasmine. "It's hidden under the sea. Do you know where it is, Lady Merlana?"

"I've heard of it, of course," the mermaid replied. "Everyone knows the legend of the Silver Shell that protects the Secret Kingdom's seas, but I don't know where to find it."

The girls exchanged anxious looks. Lady Merlana had lived under the sea for her whole life. If she didn't know where the Enchanted Object was hidden, who would?

"At least we know we're looking for a silver shell now," said Jasmine. "That's something."

"The Wise Old Manatee might be able to help," Lady Merlana said thoughtfully. "He knows everything about our undersea world."

"Where does he live?" asked Summer.

Before Lady Merlana could reply, a dark shadow fell across the seabed and the little merchildren clustered together fearfully. A tall, thin figure dressed in a black wetsuit floated down and landed in the middle of the school hall. She was wearing a diver's mask over her eyes but now she pushed it up to the top of her head and glared round.

The girls gasped in horror.

"Queen Malice!" groaned Ellie.

The Wise Old Manatee

"I heard that Pearl Shoals School was expecting a visitor for a magic show," Queen Malice said, "so here I am – a *royal* visitor! Aren't you lucky?" She smirked at the merchildren. "But your magic display didn't seem very magical."

"You're not welcome here," Jasmine said bravely. "And we're going to stop you

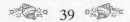

from stealing the Secret Kingdom's good magic, so everybody's spells will work properly again!"

"Oh, really?" The mean queen scooped up a handful of sand and let it run through her fingers. "Remember my hourglass? Well, time is running out. Nearly half the sand has run through already." She threw back her head and cackled loudly. "You pesky girls won't stop me this time and soon the Secret Kingdom will be mine!"

She yanked on a thick rope that hung down beside her in the water and two enormous red eyes peered down from high above them.

"What's that?" gasped Ellie, shrinking back in horror when she realised that the rope was really a massive tentacle!

"It's a giant squid,"
Queen Malice said.
"And let me tell you
something else. I'm
going to find the
Silver Shell before
you. So there!"

"You're not!" cried Summer.

"Black out the waters of the deep

And send these nincompoops to sleep!"

screeched Queen Malice. She banged her thunderbolt staff on the sandy floor, then tugged the giant squid's tentacle again. It squirted a cloud of ink into the water, turning it black. "Sweet dreams!" the queen cackled. She wrapped the tentacle around her body. "Pull me up quick, you squiddy idiot!"

The tentacle tightened and Queen Malice was whisked up and away, disappearing into the murky gloom.

"We can't let her find the Silver Shell before we do!" Summer said with a gasp.

But the squid's ink was so dark that they couldn't see where the mean queen had gone.

"Let's hurry and find the Wise Old
Manatee," suggested Trixi. But when they
turned to Lady Merlana to ask where
he lived, they found her slumped on the
bench, yawning widely.

"Are you all right?" said Jasmine
anxiously.

The mermaid yawned again and her eyelids fluttered closed. "Can't...keep... my eyes...open," she whispered sleepily.

"Queen Malice put a spell on the squid's ink and it must be making her sleepy," Trixi said. "I'll try to get rid of it so she wakes up." She tapped her ring, but the sea remained murky. "My magic's still not working." She sighed.

"We need your help, Lady Merlana," said Ellie desperately. She shook the mermaid gently, trying to wake her.

"Please tell us where to find the Wise Old Manatee," Summer begged.

Lady Merlana began to slide off the bench.

"She's going to fall," cried Ellie.

The girls quickly guided the mermaid towards a bed of soft pink sea anemones

near the bench. They looked like a row
of plump cushions. Lady Merlana settled
down with a contented sigh
and a moment
later she began
to snore gently.

"Maybe
someone else
knows where
the Wise Old
Manatee
lives,"
suggested
Jasmine.
They looked round hopefully but the
merchildren and Miss Sandy were
snuggled together, fast asleep too.

"Why aren't we asleep like everyone
else?" Jasmine asked.

"It must be our breathing bubbles," said Trixi. "The squid's ink can't reach us so Queen Malice's sleeping spell hasn't worked on us."

"Let's get out of this murky water," Ellie said. "Then we might find someone who can help us."

They kicked hard with their flippers and sped through the dark water. Soon they reached clear water and saw three large, sleek shapes moving above them.

"Dolphins!" cried Summer.

They raced to the surface and found the glossy dolphins leaping over waves and making excited clicking noises.

"Hello," they called out in musical voices, gathering around the girls.

"Can you tell us where to find the Wise Old Manatee, please?" asked Jasmine.

"We can do something even better," replied one of the dolphins, laughing with a whistling noise. "We'll take you there! Climb on our backs."

Eagerly the girls scrambled on to the dolphins' backs and held on tightly to their fins. Trixi sat in front of Summer and the dolphins set off, speeding through the water and leaving a frothy trail behind them.

"This is brilliant!" Jasmine exclaimed as they raced along.

Soon the dolphins slowed down. The girls saw what looked like a grassy field under the sea. The sea grasses were tall and they swayed in the gentle current.

"Here we are," said one of the dolphins. "The Wise Old Manatee lives in this field. But we've never met him – he's very shy."

The girls slid down from the dolphins' backs. "Thank you for the ride," said Summer, hugging her dolphin.

He flicked his tail excitedly and patted her with his fin. "Any time!" he said.

Ellie led the way into the tall grass and Jasmine, Summer and Trixi followed. When they looked back, the dolphins were waving goodbye with their flippers. "Good luck!" they squeaked.

"Thanks," the girls called back. They swam further into the field. "Hello," they called together. "Is anyone here?"

There was no answer.

"It's hard to see anything through all this tall grass," muttered Ellie.

"And we don't even know what a manatee looks like," Jasmine added.

"I do," said Summer. "They're a bit like seals, only much bigger, and very gentle. Some people call them sea cows."

"That explains why the Wise Old Manatee lives in a grassy field." Ellie giggled. "Come on, let's keep looking."

They swam in and out of the grassy seaweed, calling for the manatee.

Suddenly Jasmine spotted something large and blue moving amongst the tall grass. She peered more closely, her heart thudding with excitement. "Over here!" she cried.

Summer, Ellie and Trixi zoomed over to her. "Have you found him?" asked Trixi eagerly.

"I think so," said Jasmine. She parted

the grass with her hands and saw a whiskery blue face staring out at her. "Are you the Wise Old Manatee?" she asked hopefully.

"Maybe," he replied in a whisper. "It depends who's asking." He turned and swam away from her.

"We badly need your help," Summer

called after him. "Please come back and talk to us."

The manatee kept going. They could barely see him now through the waving sea grass.

"Can you tell us where to find the Silver Shell?" Summer cried.

The manatee stopped.

"We desperately need to find it," said Jasmine.

The manatee turned and stared at them grumpily.

"Queen Malice is trying to steal all the good magic from the Secret Kingdom," Ellie told him. "But we can stop her if we find the four Enchanted Objects and give them to King Merry."

"Why should I believe you?" asked the Wise Old Manatee, twitching his

whiskers suspiciously. "Perhaps you want
to help wicked Queen Malice."

Trixi swam right
up to the
manatee
and
pointed to
the girls'
heads.
"These
tiaras show
that the girls are
King Merry's Very Important Friends,"
she said. "And I can prove it!" She tapped
her ring and a golden bubble appeared
beside her. It grew bigger and bigger
until the girls could see someone inside it.

"It's Bobbins, King Merry's butler!"
exclaimed Jasmine.

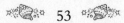

Bobbins looked up, surprised, and waved at them.

"Bother," said Trixi with a sigh. "My magic's still not working properly." She tapped her ring again and this time King Merry appeared in the bubble. "Your Majesty, please will you tell the Wise Old Manatee about our mission?" she said.

King Merry looked up in astonishment and his crown slipped down over one eye. He pushed it back up on to his head. "Please give them all the help you can, Wise Old Manatee. The

Secret Kingdom's magic is in danger!"

"Very well, Your Majesty," agreed the manatee.

The bubble vanished.

"So do you know where we can find the Silver Shell?" asked Jasmine.

"I'd like to help," said the manatee, "but I'm afraid you must work out where it is for yourselves. But if you're truly friends of the Secret Kingdom, you should be able to do it…"

The Pearls of Wisdom

The girls looked at each other in dismay. Finding the Wise Old Manatee hadn't helped them in their search at all!

"Can't you tell us anything?" said Ellie.

The manatee looked all round as though he was afraid of being overheard. "Find the three Pearls of Wisdom," he whispered. "They're hidden in this field. A

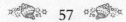

riddle is written on each pearl but only a true friend of the kingdom, who knows its waters well, will be able to answer them."

The girls exchanged relieved looks. They were *definitely* true friends of the Secret Kingdom so they should be able to solve the riddles easily.

"If you answer correctly," the manatee continued, "the pearls will glow and lead you to the Silver Shell. Good luck." He shuffled backwards and disappeared into the waving sea grass.

"Let's split up and start searching," suggested Jasmine.

They swam in different directions, scouring the sand and the sea grass for the pearls. Suddenly, Summer saw a black shape moving through the water. She shrank down, frightened that it might be a shark. As it came closer, she realised that it was something even worse. "A Storm Sprite!" she gasped.

Jasmine, Ellie and Trixi swam over to her but suddenly Storm Sprites, ugly creatures who worked for Queen Malice, were everywhere.

"Ha ha!" they jeered, pointing at the girls with their sharp fingers and sticking out their tongues.

"We heard what that silly manatee said and we're going to find the pearls before you!" sneered one of them.

"No, you're not!" cried Jasmine bravely.

Suddenly, Ellie spotted something glinting in the sand. She quickly swam towards it but before she could pick it up, a Storm Sprite grabbed it. "A Pearl of Wisdom!" he cheered.

"Give it here, bird-brain!" shouted another. He tried to snatch the pearl. "You're too silly to answer a riddle."

"Am not!" The first sprite pushed him

away and quickly read out the riddle:

"These creatures of the Snowy Seas
Keep the animals safe and well.
Shout their name out loud and clear
To find the magic Silver Shell."

The answer was so obvious that Ellie almost blurted it out. They'd met these protectors of the animals when they were searching for the Seal Keeper. Luckily, Summer placed a finger on her lips, warning Ellie to stay quiet until they had the pearl themselves.

"What's the answer then?" demanded one of the Storm Sprites.

They all gathered round the sprite holding the pearl. "How should I know?" he answered sulkily.

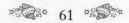

"Is it sharks?" called another.

"Or stingrays?" said a third.

The girls giggled. It was clear the Storm Sprites didn't have a clue.

"Stupid pearl!" the first sprite snapped, throwing it down on the sand. "Let's find the other ones."

The sprites splashed away, flapping their bat-like wings.

Ellie dived for the pearl and quickly scooped it up. "The answer is the ice mermaids!" she cried.

At once the pearl began to glow with soft white light.

"Well done, Ellie!" cried Summer and Jasmine.

They carried on searching for the last two pearls and Jasmine soon spotted one under a clump of sea grass. As she raced

towards it, a sprite began to chase her. "She's seen another one!" he shrieked.

He tried to push past her, but Jasmine was quicker. She snatched up the pearl, then swam away and ducked down in the tall grass.

"Where's she gone?" the sprite shouted angrily.

Keeping low so they'd be hidden by the grass, Summer, Ellie and Trixi swam across to Jasmine. Jasmine read out the riddle in a whisper:

"The tide goes in, the tide goes out,
The endless movement of the sea.
Somebody controls those tides
But do you know who she might be?"

"It's Octavia," said Jasmine. They'd

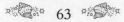

met the gentle octeo on Serenity Island when they'd been trying to get their lost talents back. Octavia used her eight legs to conduct the islanders, and their gentle music calmed the Secret Kingdom's tides.

The pearl began to glow and the girls and Trixi smiled excitedly at each other. There was only one more Pearl of Wisdom to find!

They searched again, swimming close to the sandy seabed so the Storm Sprites wouldn't see them. Spotting a movement, Summer swam over for a closer look and found a crab scuttling through the sea grass. Nearby was a shiny object half-hidden in the sand. It was the last pearl!

Gasping with excitement, Summer picked it up eagerly. "Ellie, Jasmine, Trixi – quick!" she called.

They came racing over. Summer held out the pearl on the palm of her hand and read out the riddle:

"This special sandy sparkly place
Is such a lovely sight,
Especially when fairies come
Upon Midsummer's night."

"It's Glitter Beach," cried Summer. A tiny pinprick of light appeared in the middle of the pearl. It grew gradually bigger until the whole pearl was glowing brightly.

"We've done it!" cried Ellie, twirling round excitedly. Suddenly, she saw two Storm Sprites heading their way. "Look out!" she warned, but it was too late. One of the sprites snatched the shining pearl out of Summer's hand.

"We'll find the Silver Shell before you!"
he jeered.

"Give that back!" shouted Jasmine. She
grabbed hold of the pearl but the Storm
Sprite wouldn't let go. He pulled hard,
but Jasmine held on tight.

Ellie caught hold of Jasmine's waist
to help her, but another Storm Sprite
joined the sprite holding the pearl. The

sprites yanked it hard, dragging the girls through the water. Summer put her arms round Ellie's middle and tugged both of her friends back, but by now more sprites had joined in.

"You can't have the pearl," panted Ellie, glaring at the sprites.

They sneered and went on pulling. It was a tug of war between the girls and the sprites, but Ellie, Summer and Jasmine

were determined to win.

"Let go!" yelled one of the Storm Sprites.

"Never!" Jasmine cried, tugging the pearl free of the Storm Sprites. She suddenly felt her fingers slipping a little on the pearl. Jasmine tried to tighten her grip, but it slid from her fingers.

Jasmine gasped as the pearl began to float away through the water. Chasing after the drifting pearl, the girls saw with dismay that they were now at the edge of a deep, dark trench. The pearl plunged into it and went on sinking.

The grass rippled and the Wise Old Manatee appeared. "Oh dear!" he groaned. "The Pearl of Wisdom has fallen into the Atlantis Trench, the deepest part of all the Secret Kingdom's seas."

"Ha, ha!" jeered the Storm Sprites. "You'll never find the Enchanted

Object now!" they taunted, before swimming off.

Horrified, the girls stared into the dark water. The pearl had almost vanished into the gloom. Only a tiny glimmer of light still showed

and it was growing smaller by the second.

"How are we going to track down the Silver Shell now?" whispered Summer. She was close to tears. They'd found the three pearls and solved all the riddles but the horrible Storm Sprites had ruined everything anyway.

Ellie put her arm around Summer. "We'll find a way," she said, but she didn't sound too sure.

"I'll try my magic," said Trixi. She tapped her pixie ring and the girls watched hopefully as a few golden sparkles danced around it before fizzling out. Trixi sighed, "My magic's not strong enough to bring it back."

The girls exchanged anxious looks. The pearl was just a speck of pale light now. "There has to be a way of getting it

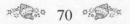

back," said Jasmine.

The girls thought hard, desperately trying to think of solution.

"Maybe we can ask the dolphins to get it back for us," suggested Ellie hopefully.

"I'm afraid not," the Wise Old Manatee replied. "Nobody is brave enough to go into the Atlantis Trench."

Jasmine looked at her friends expectantly, and after a moment they all nodded.

"Well, *we* are!" exclaimed Jasmine. "Let's go!"

◌Into the Darkness◌

Jasmine dived down into the dark water.

"Wait for us!" cried Ellie and Summer together. They plunged into the Atlantis Trench after Jasmine, with Trixi following close behind them.

Down, down, down they swam. It was so dark they couldn't see anything, not even each other, and there was nothing to guide them but the faint light of the Pearl of Wisdom. It was sinking fast.

Summer shivered and reached out into
the dark, feeling for her friends' hands.
She longed to be able to see where
they were going. Ellie gave her hand a
reassuring squeeze, then Jasmine took her
other hand and they stuck close together
as they swam after the pearl.

"We've got to be brave," Jasmine said.

Still they swam deeper. Ellie was
beginning to think the trench might go
down and down forever when her flipper
touched solid ground. "This must be the
bottom," she said.

"Thank goodness!" Summer exclaimed.
"Now we'll be able to find the pearl."

The girls and Trixi peered into the
darkness, trying to catch sight of it.
Jasmine spotted a faint yellow light a
long way off. It seemed to be moving

up and down. "There it is!" she cried. "Come on."

She pulled her friends towards it, but Ellie spotted a distant pink glow and stopped her. "It's the other way," she said, pointing.

Now they noticed more tiny twinkling lights all around them. They were every colour of the rainbow and growing brighter by the second. "What are they, Trixi?" asked Summer. "They look like fairy lights."

"I don't know," Trixi replied. "But hopefully they'll help us see where we're going."

The lights came closer and the girls saw that they were shining from lanterns of all shapes and sizes that bobbed from the heads of small, shimmering fish. "Lantern fish!" Trixi cried. "That's exactly what we need!"

The fish reached the girls and darted around them excitedly. "I think they're welcoming us," said Summer, stroking the fish closest to her. As they gracefully waved their fins at her, their colourful lanterns swayed from side to side and lit up the rocks and coral nearby. Beneath the girls' feet, the sand glittered as though it was scattered with tiny jewels.

"What an amazing place!" gasped

Jasmine, reaching out to touch a
rock made of thousands of twinkling
diamonds.

"We should be able to find the pearl
easily now that there's light," Summer
added happily.

They began to search again, swimming
slowly through the soaring, gem-
encrusted walls of the trench. Looking
round for the missing pearl, they ducked
under glistening arches and swam
through clumps of feathery seaweed as
tall as trees. The lantern fish followed
them as they swam so that the glittering
rocks appeared to be constantly changing
colour.

They saw wonderful striped giant crabs
scuttling along the seabed, and jellyfish
whose tentacles only tickled as they

glided past. A family of seahorses bobbed by, their tails curling and uncurling. The babies darted over to the girls and gently touched their noses in greeting before swimming on. Summer wished she could follow them, but they had to keep searching for the pearl.

"I can see it!" cried Ellie suddenly. She pointed to a line of jagged white rocks that marked the mouth of a dark cave. The pearl was lying next to the biggest rock.

"Well spotted!" Jasmine exclaimed.

The girls and Trixi swam swiftly towards the cave, but the lantern fish shrank back.

"Please come with us," Summer urged. "We need your lights."

The little fish began to flash their lanterns on and off. They swam round the girls in a tight circle and tried to nudge them back the way they'd come.

"I think they want to tell us something," said Summer anxiously.

Trixi tapped her ring and chanted:

*"Pixie magic, hear my wish
And let us understand these fish."*

A few silver sparkles fizzed out of the ring, but they faded almost at once.

"Oh, dear!" Trixi sighed. "If only my magic would work."

"What shall we do?" said Summer as the lantern fish bumped against them.

"The manatee said the Pearls of Wisdom would lead us to the Silver Shell," Jasmine pointed out, "so we've got to get it."

"Jasmine's right," agreed Ellie. "We'll never find the shell without the pearl."

The girls swam cautiously towards it. The lantern fish were blinking their lights on and off urgently. Summer was sure that the fish were trying to tell them

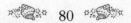

something, but the sooner they picked up the pearl the sooner they could swim away from the cave.

They'd almost reached the cave when another row of white rocks came crashing down from high above their heads.

"What's happened?" Ellie gasped, shocked.

"It's a dragon fish!" cried Trixi in terror. "This isn't a cave at all – it's his mouth. The white rocks are his teeth!"

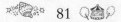

"He's swallowed the pearl!" wailed
Jasmine in dismay.

Summer stared at the massive creature.
Its head and body were like scaly purple
hills that almost filled the trench from
side to side, and its tail stretched so far
into the distance that its end was hidden
in the darkness.

It had four
stumpy legs,
two huge
fins and
enormous
webbed
feet.

The
dragon
fish lunged
towards the

girls and Trixi and gave a ferocious roar.
A torrent of bubbles poured out of its
mouth and sent the girls whooshing back
as though they were on a water slide.

"At least it doesn't breathe fire," Jasmine
said as they tumbled head over heels
through the water.

The bubbles began to pop and the girls came to a stop in the middle of the shoal of lantern fish. "Thanks for trying to warn us," Summer said to them. "But we really need to get that pearl back."

"We've lost it again," said Ellie in a gloomy voice. "What are we going to do?"

"I don't think the dragon fish will give it up any time soon," Jasmine said sadly.

Summer glanced back at the sea monster. "Dragons are meant to guard treasure," she said thoughtfully. "Maybe it wasn't an accident that the Pearl of Wisdom fell down here. Maybe it *has* led us to the Silver Shell and the dragon fish is guarding it."

"Of course!" cried Jasmine. "The shell must be close or the pearl wouldn't have

brought us here. We need to look for it."

They swam towards the monster again, hoping to get past it, but it snapped its massive teeth at them and drove them back in another torrent of bubbles.

"This is hopeless," sighed Ellie.

"I'll distract it," Jasmine offered. "Then you two and Trixi can search behind it."

"Are you sure?" asked Summer anxiously.

"Of course," insisted Jasmine. "I'll be fine." Summoning all her courage, she swam towards the dragon fish again. It turned its head to watch her, its green eyes fierce.

"Come on," Ellie whispered. "Let's sneak past quickly while it's looking the other way."

The sea monster snapped its sharp teeth

at Jasmine but she dodged them easily, then swam towards it again.

"We'll need some light," said Trixi.

A pretty orange lantern fish darted forward. Trixi sat on his back so she could steer him to where they needed his light. Summer and Ellie slipped past the monster, taking care not to splash and attract its attention. Trixi followed close behind on the fish, its lantern filling the trench with yellow light. They glided above the monster's massive humped back, looking left and right as they tried to spot the shell, but there was no sign of it anywhere.

"Let's look around its feet," suggested Summer in a low voice.

They swam down to the seabed and shone the lantern fish's light on the

monster's huge webbed feet, but the Silver Shell wasn't there either.

"Let's try near its tail," Ellie whispered. The monster jerked suddenly and they heard its teeth clash together. Summer,

Ellie and Trixi all froze.

"I hope Jasmine's okay," said Summer nervously. She hated to think of their friend having to face the monster alone.

"The sooner we find the Silver Shell, the sooner we can all get out of here," said Trixi.

They swam up, high above the dragon fish's tail.

"What's that?" asked Ellie suddenly. The lantern light had picked out something shining near the tip of its tail. As she swam closer, she saw that it was a large spiralling

conch shell with a wide opening along
one side. It was made of gleaming silver.

"The Silver Shell!" Summer cried.
"We've found it!"

·Queen Malice's Secret·

Ellie scooped up the Silver Shell. "Let's find Jasmine and get out of here as we can," she said. She and Summer raced back, with Trixi riding close behind them on the lantern fish.

They slipped past the dragon fish's enormous body, then stopped and stared in horror. The creature had caught the tip of Jasmine's flipper in its mouth! She was

struggling to pull it free, but the monster wouldn't let her go.

Ellie hurriedly set the shell down on the sand, then she and Summer sped over to Jasmine. Their hearts thumped wildly as Summer took Jasmine's hands and Ellie grabbed her flipper. They pulled with all their might and suddenly the front of her flipper snapped off.

Jasmine was free!

Turning, they swam away as fast as they could. "Is it chasing us?" gasped Jasmine.

Summer glanced back over her shoulder. To her relief, the dragon fish was swimming away in the opposite direction, its webbed feet paddling furiously and its huge scaly body shimmering in the lantern light. "It's going!" she exclaimed in astonishment.

"I thought it would try to get the Silver Shell back," said Ellie, sounding puzzled.

They stared after the enormous creature but it had already vanished into the darkness.

"So you found the shell?" asked Jasmine.

"Yes," Summer replied happily. "I left it just over here."

They swam quickly to where Summer had set it down, but it wasn't there.

"What's happened to it?" Ellie cried, peering round in surprise.

"Looking for this?" cackled a shrill, familiar voice.

The girls spun round in the water. "Queen Malice!" groaned Summer. "Oh no!"

"Oh yes!" shrieked the mean queen.

"So that's why the dragon fish swam away so suddenly," Jasmine said. "It must have been frightened of Queen Malice."

The queen held up the Silver Shell. "Thank you so much for doing all the hard work for me. I'd never have found this if it hadn't been for you."

"Give it back," Jasmine said. They all swam over to the wicked queen.

"We found it."

The queen laughed nastily. "I will
NOT give it back."

Suddenly the girls found themselves
surrounded by Storm Sprites riding on
the backs of large black eels. As the eels
lashed their tails from side to side, the
water began to fizz. "Don't
get too close to my
Agony Eels,"

warned Queen Malice. "If their tails zap you, you won't be very happy about it."

A large whiskery catfish came swimming along the bottom of the trench. One of the eels stretched its tail towards him and fired a bolt of fizzing blue bubbles that surrounded the catfish. The poor creature's whiskers stood on end and a shimmering blue light flickered through its scales.

The catfish shot away in alarm.

Queen Malice threw back her head and roared with laughter. "He won't come back in a hurry," she hooted.

The girls looked at each other anxiously. The Agony Eels were scary, but they knew they couldn't let Queen Malice escape with the Silver Shell.

Bravely, the girls ignored the eels and

the sprites and closed in on the mean
queen. Jasmine made a grab for the Silver
Shell, but Queen Malice threw it over her
head to one of the sprites. He tucked it
under his arm and darted away. "Can't
catch me!" he jeered.

"Come on!" cried Ellie.

They chased after the Storm Sprite, swimming as fast as they could, but as the girls began to catch up he threw the shell to another sprite. Now all the sprites joined in the game, tossing the shell back and forth between them.

"Over here!" they called.

"No, throw it to me!"

The girls swam this way and that,

avoiding the eels' tails which sent streams
of fizzing bubbles towards
them whenever they
got too close.

"There are
too many of
them. We're
never going
to get the
shell back this
way," panted
Jasmine. "We've
got to think of
another plan."

They stopped chasing the sprites and
formed a tight huddle. "I've got an idea,"
said Ellie. "Remember our adventure at
the Petal Parade?"

Summer and Jasmine nodded.

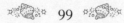

"And do you remember the secret we learned about Queen Malice?" Ellie asked.

"She's afraid of the dark!" Summer replied.

"Exactly," continued Ellie. "If the lantern fish turn off their lights, it might scare the queen into giving back the Silver Shell."

"That's a great idea," said Jasmine. "But how will we tell the lantern fish what we want them to do?"

"My magic should work now that the Silver Shell is nearby," Trixi said. She tapped her ring and whispered:

"Let the fish know what I mean
So we can beat the nasty queen."

Multi-coloured sparkles poured out of her ring and whirled around the lantern fish. They turned towards Trixi.

"When I count to three, please turn off your lights," she said.

The fish rippled their fins and the girls held their breath. Had they understood?

"One…two…three!" said Trixi.

Suddenly every light was suddenly switched off and the trench was plunged into deep darkness. Only the Silver Shell gave off a soft glow.

Queen Malice screamed. "Turn your lights back on," she begged.

"Hand over the shell first," said Summer. "Then the lights will go on again."

"Quickly, Storm Sprites!" the queen yelled. "Give her the shell."

A Storm Sprite thrust the Silver Shell
into Summer's hands and on Trixi's
command the lantern fishes' lights flicked
on again.

Queen Malice looked pale, but very
angry. She thumped her lightning staff on
the sea floor and her
hourglass magically
appeared. "You
may have
cheated me out
of the Silver
Shell," she said
in a furious
voice, "but look
how much sand
you have already
lost."

The girls gasped.

More than half of the black sand had run into the lower part of the hourglass.

"You'll never find the last two Enchanted Objects before it runs out completely!" she sneered, as she and the Storm Sprites raced away on their Agony Eels. "And then the kingdom will be mine!"

"Oh no," said Trixi, looking worried.

"We'll never let that happen," Summer reassured her.

"Never," Ellie echoed firmly.

"Don't worry," Jasmine said. "We've stopped Queen Malice before – and we'll do it again!"

Mermaid Magic

Summer held up the Silver Shell. "We've got the second Enchanted Object," she said. "So we are halfway to breaking Queen Malice's spell."

"Let's take it back to Pearl Shoals," suggested Jasmine.

They swam up and out of the trench. The Silver Shell lit their way through the darkness. Fish and other sea creatures

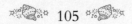

gathered to watch them swim by, waving their fins and blowing bubbles in the water.

"Goodbye, everyone," called Trixi. "Thank you for helping us find the Silver Shell."

They soon reached the school and were relieved to see that the water was crystal clear again. The merchildren were waking up, stretching their arms and tails, yawning and rubbing their eyes.

Lady Merlana swam over to meet them. "You found the Silver Shell!" she cried. "Well done, girls!"

Miss Sandy hurried over. "The children would like to try showing you their spells again, Lady Merlana," she said. "The sea feels full of mermaid magic now the shell is here."

"That would be lovely," said Lady Merlana. "Will you join us, girls?"

"Yes, please," said Ellie, Jasmine and Summer together. Once more they sat down on the seaweed-cushioned bench beside Lady Merlana, while Trixi perched her leaf on Jasmine's shoulder.

The merchildren swam into the centre of the hall and bowed to their guests. "The rainbow fish spell," announced Miss Sandy, as a shoal of silver fish swam in into the hall.

All the merchildren joined hands and sang the spell that had created the pufferfish before. But this time a ball of silver light appeared around. It grew bigger and bigger, then suddenly burst into colourful sparkles like a firework display! As the sparkles touched the fish,

their scales changed to shimmering reds,
blues, greens, purples and yellows.

The girls clapped in delight as a
rainbow of fish raced around the hall,
then out through one of the windows.

"Bravo!" called Lady Merlana.

"Now for our flower spell," Miss Sandy said. The merchildren linked hands again and sang:

"Flowers are a joy for all
So let them grow inside our walls."

The water around them began to ripple, then flowers magically grew from the glittering sandy floor and pearl walls. They opened their petals wide, filling the hall with colour.

"That's beautiful!" exclaimed Jasmine.

"And now for our final spell," said Miss Sandy. The merchildren gathered in front of the girls and Lady Merlana and sang another spell:

"Everyone deserves a treat
So bring us lovely food to eat."

There was a brilliant flash and a table suddenly appeared. It was piled high with delicious-looking food. The girls applauded and Miss Sandy looked very proud. "Please help yourselves," she said. "There's plenty for everyone."

"How can we eat with our breathing bubbles on?" asked Summer.

"Leave it to me," Trixi said. She tapped her ring and the bubbles popped. "The Silver Shell's made my magic strong enough to let you breathe without them."

The girls tucked into sweet sandy biscuits, delicate seashell-shaped cakes, and glasses of frothy sea-berry juice.

"Amazing!" said Ellie, licking her lips.

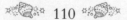

When everyone had eaten their fill,
Summer said, "We really should get
the Silver Shell back to King Merry's
Enchanted Palace now."

Jasmine nodded. "It will be safe from
Queen Malice there."

"No problem," said Trixi.

She tapped her pixie ring and chanted:

*"The Silver Shell's a precious thing
So send it swiftly to the king."*

Suddenly the shell vanished.

"How will we know that King Merry's
got the shell?" Summer asked anxiously.

Trixi tapped her ring again. A golden
bubble appeared. It grew bigger and
bigger and now they could see King
Merry inside it. He was holding the shell

and staring at it in astonishment. "Well
I never!" he exclaimed. Then he glanced
up and saw the girls. "Thank you!" he
called, beaming. "I'll keep the Silver Shell
with the Charmed Heart for safekeeping.
And I'll send for you girls again as soon
as I have an idea about where the third
Enchanted Object might be."

"We'll come straightaway to find it,"
promised Jasmine.

The bubble popped.

"It's time for you girls to go home
now," Trixi said.

"Thank you for restoring magic to
the Secret Kingdom's waters," said Lady
Merlana, hugging each of the girls.

The girls said goodbye to Miss Sandy
and their new merchild friends, then they
joined hands. Trixi tapped her ring and

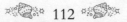

the water around them began to glitter
and swirl. Soon, a sparkling whirlpool
was spinning around them. The girls felt
themselves being lifted up through the
water. "Goodbye, everyone. Goodbye,
Trixi," they called.

The next moment they found
themselves back in Summer's bedroom.
Time had stood still while they were
gone.

"What an adventure!" exclaimed Jasmine. "And we're completely dry. You'd never guess we were under the sea a few seconds ago!"

The kitchen timer dinged. "Our biscuits must be ready," said Ellie. She hastily stuffed the Magic Box into Jasmine's backpack, then they ran

downstairs to the kitchen.

Summer carefully slid the trays of biscuits out of the oven and they put them on a rack to cool.

"They smell delicious!" said Jasmine.

Summer helped herself to a mermaid-shaped biscuit. "Yummy!" she said. Then she grinned at Ellie and Jasmine. "But nothing is sweeter than knowing we've beaten Queen Malice again!"

In the next Secret Kingdom adventure, Ellie, Summer and Jasmine make a

Genie Wish

Read on for a sneak peek...

A Garden Riddle

"Isn't this fun?" Jasmine Smith said happily to her two best friends, Ellie Macdonald and Summer Hammond. The three girls were spending the afternoon making pictures using some tubes of sparkly, coloured sand and glue that Ellie had bought at the craft shop.

Ellie nodded. She had drawn an outline

in glue and sprinkled sand on. Now she gently shook the loose bits of sand on to the newspaper covering the table. "I love making sand pictures."

"You love anything to do with art," Summer said with a smile. "And you're so good at it too. Your picture is amazing."

"Thanks," said Ellie. Summer and Jasmine had both made quite simple pictures with the sand and glue – Summer's was a cat and Jasmine's was a microphone – but Ellie's was far more complicated. She had drawn a beautiful palace with pink pointy turrets and a grand entrance.

"It's just like the Royal Palace in the Secret Kingdom," Jasmine said, looking over Ellie's shoulder.

"Shh!" Ellie said. "Mum might hear."

The three friends shared an incredible secret. They were the only people that knew about the Secret Kingdom – an amazing, magical land that was filled with wonderful creatures like pixies, unicorns, mermaids, elves and fairies. It was ruled by the jolly King Merry, and Ellie, Summer and Jasmine had visited it lots of times.

"Do you think King Merry has worked out where the last two Enchanted Objects are yet?" Jasmine whispered.

"Probably not, or he would have sent us a message in the Magic Box," said Ellie.

"I hope he figures out where they are soon," said Summer. "Then we can go and help him find them!"

The girls were in the middle of one of their Secret Kingdom adventures. The king's wicked sister, Queen Malice, had cast a horrible spell, which was making all the magic in the Secret Kingdom slowly drain away. The only way to stop her was to find the four special Enchanted Objects that were hidden around the kingdom. Together the objects' magic could reverse the queen's nasty spell – but time was running out. If they didn't find them all before the sand ran through Queen Malice's cursed hourglass then all the magic in the Secret Kingdom would vanish forever.

"At least we've found the Charmed Heart and the Silver Shell," said Ellie. "I wonder what the last two objects will be."

"And *where* they'll be," added Jasmine.

"Perhaps we should go and check on the Magic Box to see if there's a message from

King Merry," said Summer. "It's in your room, isn't it, Ellie?"

"Yes, it's in my bag, inside my wardrobe under some—" Ellie broke off as Molly, her four-year-old sister, came charging into the kitchen. Her green eyes were wide and her red curls were bouncing on her shoulders.

"Ellie!" she gasped. "I just went into your room and there's a light shining from your wardrobe! Quickly! You've got to come and see!"

Ellie, Summer and Jasmine jumped up in alarm. The glow Molly saw must have been coming from the Magic Box – it always sparkled and shone when King Merry sent them a message.

"A shining light? In my wardrobe? Oh, don't worry about that, Moll," Ellie said hurriedly. "It's just…just…"

"I bet it's that torch I lent you, Ellie," Jasmine said quickly. "Do you remember? You put it into your bag when we were at school."

"That's right," said Ellie gratefully. "I must have left it switched on. Silly me."

"Oh," said Molly, disappointed at such a boring explanation.

"Hey, Molly have you seen our pictures and this cool glitter?" said Summer, holding up some pink sparkly sand. She had two little brothers and she knew how much they loved anything to do with arts and crafts.

"Oh, wow!' said Molly, going over. "It's really pretty."

"Would you like to make a picture?" Ellie said. "Maybe you could draw a person or do some patterns."

"Oh, yes please!" said Molly.

"Here you go then," said Ellie, putting some paper and glue in front of her. "Use the glue to make your picture and then scatter the sand on top. Just don't make too much mess or Mum will get cross. We'll just pop upstairs to turn that torch off and then we'll come back and help you."

Read

Genie Wish

to find out what
happens next!

Have you read all the books in Series Seven?

When the last grain of sand falls in Queen Malice's cursed hourglass, magic will be lost from the Secret Kingdom forever!
Can Ellie, Summer and Jasmine find all the Enchanted Objects and break the spell?

Keep all your dreams and wishes safe in this gorgeous Secret Kingdom Notebook!

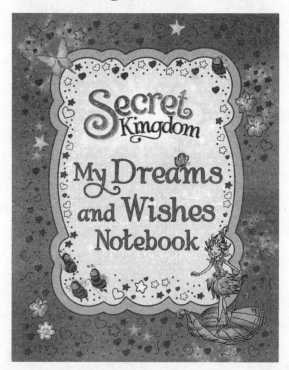

Includes a party planner, diary, dream journal and lots more!

Out now!

Look out for the latest special!

Out now!

Queen Malice's spell on the Magic Hourglass is making everything in the Secret Kingdom go wonky!

Can you help the girls put things right by colouring in the picture below and bring back the good magic to the Secret Kingdom?

Competition!

Those naughty Storm Sprites are up to no good again. They have trampled through this book and left muddy footprints on one of the pages!

Did you spot them while you were reading this book?

Can you find the pages where the cheeky sprites have left their footprints in each of the four books in series 7?
When you have found all four sets of footprints, go online and tell us which pages they are on to enter the competition at

www.secretkingdombooks.com

We will put all of the correct entries into a draw and select a winner to receive a special Secret Kingdom goody bag!

Alternatively send entries to:
Secret Kingdom, Series 7 Competition
Orchard Books, Carmelite House, 50 Victoria Embankment,
London, EC4Y 0DZ

Don't forget to add your name and address.

Good luck!

Closing date: 29th February 2016

Secret Kingdom

A magical world of
friendship and fun!

Join the Secret Kingdom Club at

www.secretkingdombooks.com

and enjoy games, sneak peeks and lots more!

You'll find great activities, competitions, stories
and games, plus a special newsletter for
Secret Kingdom friends!